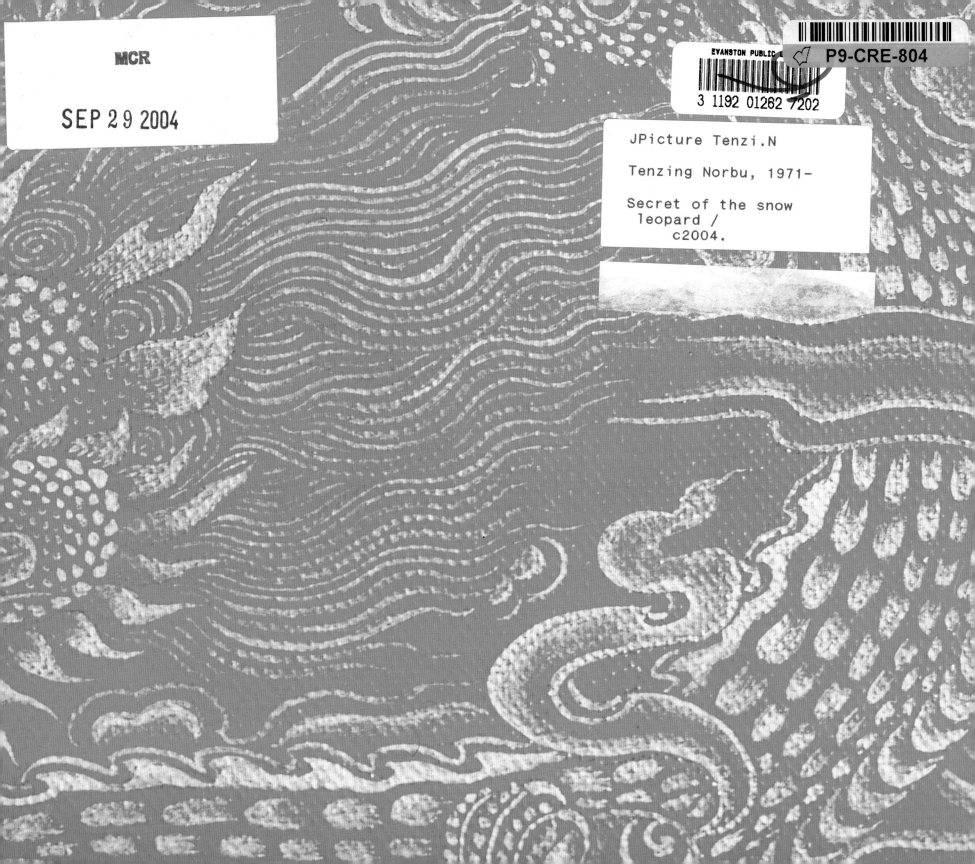

Copyright © 2002 Éditions MILAN/France
English text copyright © 2004 by Groundwood Books

First published in French in 2002 by Éditions Milan as *Himalaya: Le Chemin du Léopard*.

French text by Stéphane Frattini, inspired by the original sceenplay by Eric Valli and Olivier Dazat, with the collaboration of Jean-Claude Guillebaud, Louis Gardel, Nathalie Azoulai and Jacques Perrin

First published in English in 2004 by Groundwood Books

Translation and adaptation by Shelley Tanaka

Groundwood Books / Douglas & McIntyre
720 Bathurst Street, Suite 500, Toronto, Ontario M5S 2R4

Distributed in the USA by Publishers Group West
1700 Fourth Street, Berkeley, CA 94710

We acknowledge for their financial support of our publishing program the Government of Ontario through the Ontario Media Development Corporation's Ontario Book Initiative.

National Library of Canada Cataloguing in Publication
Tenzing, Norbu.
Secret of the Snow Leopard / by Tenzing Norbu, Lama with Stéphane Frattini
Translation of: Himalaya: le chemin du léopard.
ISBN 0-88899-544-X
1. Snow leopard–Juvenile fiction. I. Frattini, Stéphane. II. Title.
PZ7.T3589Se 2004   j843'.92   C2003-905953-7

Printed and bound in China by Everbest Printing Co. Ltd.

TENZING NORBU LAMA
with STÉPHANE FRATTINI

SECRET OF THE
Snow Leopard

A GROUNDWOOD BOOK • DOUGLAS & MCINTYRE • TORONTO VANCOUVER BERKELEY

It was evening. One by one, the high valleys of Dolpo filled with shadow.

"Tsering!" Pema called to her son.

The young boy took aim at the shoulder bone of a sheep that he had propped against the wall. His bow had once belonged to Lhapka, his father.

"If I hit it," Tsering said, "the summer rains will start tomorrow!"

Holding his breath, he released the arrow.

He missed. Again.

"My father would be ashamed of me," Tsering fumed as he climbed back up to the village.

Before he died, Lhapka had been the village chief, the leader of the salt caravans, loved and respected by everyone.

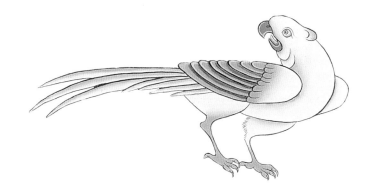

Tsering knelt by the fire and helped his mother prepare the meal. He looked up as Karma, his stepfather, came into the house.

"Tondrup is sick," Karma said, his face grim. "Nothing is making him better. He wants me to take him to the monastery. We will leave tomorrow morning."

Tondrup was the amchi, the village healer. Half doctor, half wise man, he was very important to the Dolpo-pa.

"I want to come, too!" cried Tsering.

Karma looked at Pema doubtfully.

"Go ahead," she said. "Don't worry about me." Pema placed her hand gently on her round stomach. She was expecting a baby soon.

At dawn they prepared to leave. Tondrup shivered in the cold, or perhaps it was the fever. Karma arranged wool blankets on the back of the strongest yak to make a seat for him. Two other yaks carried sacks of barley and wheat to offer to the lamas at the monastery.

"Take good care of Tsering," murmured Pema. "His heart has been so angry lately…"

"I'll watch over him as if he were my own son," Karma promised.

On the second day the travelers passed the foot of the mountain pass where Lhapka had died.

"I want to go up there!" said Tsering. "I want to climb the pass. It will be faster if we go that way!"

"No," Karma said. "It's too dangerous. Your father tried to take that shortcut and he fell to his death because of it."

So Tsering was forced to give up, but he kept looking back, his heart tight with longing.

In the heat and the dust, the yaks slowly skirted the mountain.

Suddenly, Tondrup cried weakly, "Look! A snow leopard! Up there behind the rocks!"

The others all looked up, but they saw nothing.

"You were dreaming," Karma said. "The fever is making you imagine things."

ཕྱུ་ནུ་ལ་གཟིགས་པ།

After three days, they finally saw the roofs of the monastery on the horizon.

"At last!" Tondrup murmured, at the end of his strength.

That night they were received by Rimpoché, the great lama. Tsering was awed by the old man's piercing gaze.

The lama threw three little dice again and again. Then he consulted a book for a long time.

"An evil demon has hold of you," he said to Tondrup at last. "We will conduct a ceremony to chase it away. Karma and Tsering will participate, too!"

The lama handed Tsering a bowl of buckwheat paste.

"Rub this on your face," he said. "Then mix it with a bit of saliva and a few hairs from your head. And add a little of that dirt from your hands, too," the old man said slyly.

With the paste he made a small figurine of a young boy. Then he placed it beside the fire to dry along with figurines of Tondrup and Karma.

The ceremony took place in the big room of the

monastery. The voices of the lamas rose to the slow beating of a drum. As the hours passed, the rhythm quickened, and the sound echoed over the mountains.

Suddenly there was silence. Rimpoché stood up. He rushed out of the room carrying the three figurines. Then he threw them into a mountain creek. They would be carried downstream, and the demon would follow them until the end of time.

ཆེན་པོ་ཧེ་རུ་ཀ་རྗེ་ལ། ང་ཚོ་སྲུང་ཇེ་གསུམ་མོ་ཡིན།

After several days of rest and prayer, Tondrup was indeed feeling much better.

Karma decided to start for home. He was in a hurry to get back to Pema.

"Your knots are not tight enough," he said, as he watched Tsering trying to load the packs on the back of a yak. "I'll do it."

"No!" Tsering protested. "I want to do it myself. I must be worthy of my father!"

"Your father! Always your father!" Karma replied sharply.

He regretted his words immediately, but it was too late. Tsering, furious, had already turned his back to him.

The next evening, to make up for losing his temper, Karma decided to make camp at the foot of the pass where Tsering's father had lost his life. Tondrup said prayers for Lhapka.

"Remember," he told Tsering. "Everything that lives must die in order to be reborn."

But the young boy said nothing. His mind was churning. He had made a decision, and he would not turn back. He remembered what his grandfather had once told him. "When you are faced with two paths," the old man had said, "always choose the most difficult."

A few hours before dawn, Tsering got up quietly, put on his boots and left the camp by the pale light of a thin crescent moon.

"I am going to climb the pass!" he said to himself.

But his throat was dry and his heart was beating a bit too quickly.

Karma was furious when he woke up and discovered that Tsering had disappeared.

"That foolish boy! How dare he!" he shouted.

"There's no time to lose," Tondrup said. "We must go and look for him."

"No," Karma replied. "You rest here. It will be faster if I go alone. If everything goes well, I'll bring him back in a few hours. If not…"

But he did not finish his sentence. Two years earlier he had gone through these very same motions when he looked for Tsering's father.

Tsering walked for hours without stopping. The path was narrow and treacherous. In places it disappeared entirely under masses of fallen rock.

He wondered whether his father had lost his footing on one of these rocks.

Suddenly, his heart leapt into his chest. A leopard was sitting right in the middle of the path, scarcely a stone's throw away.

Stiff with fear, Tsering hardly dared to breathe. Then he spotted a hollow in the face of the cliff just above him. He quickly scrambled up into the unexpected shelter.

གནད་རྐྱེན་ཉི་ཤུ།

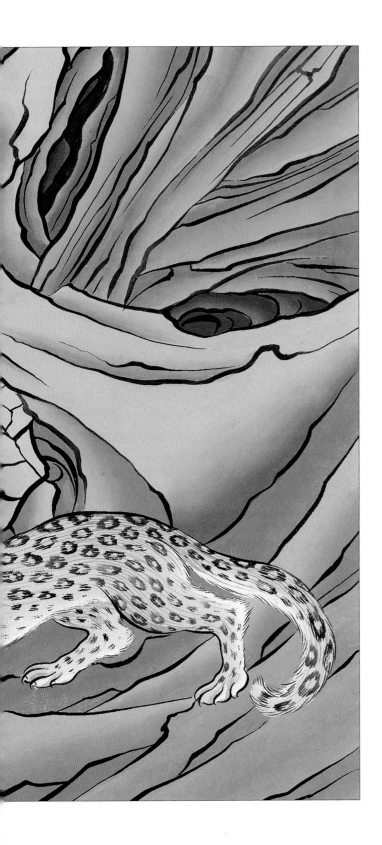

To his astonishment he found himself at the entrance to a huge cave. And all around him the walls were inscribed with holy inscriptions, the letters worn and faded.

A hermit must have lived here, Tsering thought. Perhaps one of the first inhabitants of Dolpo! Some of these wise men could fly across the sky like vultures.

Down below, the cat had started to move. The leopard's muscles rolled under its thick coat, and its long tail flicked back and forth like a whip.

At the mouth of the cave, the animal lifted its round head and stared at Tsering with icy, pale eyes. Tsering's whole body was flooded with panic.

"I'm going to die here," he groaned, huddling on the ground of the cave, as the leopard growled.

Suddenly Tsering was seized by a fierce anger. He was filled with rage at the unfairness of it all, the stupid mountains, the whole world. Without thinking, he grabbed a rock and rose up.

"Go away!" he screamed. "Leave me alone! I want to climb the pass!"

He threw the rock. It hit the side of the leopard. The animal arched its back. It bared its teeth and snarled.

"Go on! Go away!"

This time Tsering threw a whole handful of rocks. One hit the leopard on the head, and the cat sprang back.

"I am stronger than you!" Tsering screamed.

And at that the big cat suddenly turned and bounded away.

Tsering let out a long sigh.

"Thank you," he said, and he gently brushed his finger over the mysterious writings on the cave wall.

Down below, Karma was making his way up the pass when he noticed a tiny figure on the side of the mountain.

It was Tsering, and he was alive.

When Karma finally reached the top of the pass, he found the young boy sitting in the sun, rubbing his aching feet. He had hung a prayer flag on a rocky cairn nearby. It waved gaily in the wind, releasing his prayers to the gods.

"You did it," Karma said, sitting near Tsering. "Lhapka did not get this far. I found his body much lower, near the cave."

"So it was there," murmured Tsering.

He hesitated for an instant, but did not say any more.

The leopard would be a secret — a last secret between him and his father.

"There you are!" said Tondrup happily, when the two returned to the camp. "I prepared tea. I knew you would succeed."

"Tsering is the one who succeeded," Karma said. "He proved that the pass can be used after all. From now on the salt caravans will go that way."

As he spoke, he noticed that Tsering was beaming with happiness, and he suddenly realized that the round face of the boy was already becoming the face of a young man.

One day, he thought, Tsering would be chief of the Dolpo-pa.

As the three men settled down for the night, the first summer rain began to fall, filling the air with wonderful smells.

By the next day, tiny green shoots had begun to appear between the gray rocks. Two days later, the travelers finally arrived home.

Everyone in the village ran to greet them. Pema was one of the first. In her arms she held a baby with big round eyes and coppery skin.

"It's a girl!" she said. "A beautiful little girl!"

Tsering and Karma ran toward her as the people of Dolpo noisily crowded around them. They were happy to share their joy and celebrate the recovery of Tondrup, their precious amchi.

"Lha gyalo!" they cried. "The gods are victorious!"

Some weeks later, harvest time came. Early one morning, before leaving for the fields, Karma handed Tsering an object wrapped in cloth.

"Here," he said. "I made this for you."

Tsering unwrapped it and cried out with joy. It was a bow, a magnificent bow, too. It was even more beautiful than his father's!

He ran at once to the bottom of the village, to the little stone wall that was lit up by the first rays of the rising sun.

Then, with his heart calm and at peace, he slowly raised his bow, took aim at the sheep bone and released his arrow…

Tenzing Norbu Lama was born in 1971 in a little village in Dolpo, a remote region high in the Himalayas in Nepal. He grew up surrounded by the drawings of his father and his grandfather. The men of his family have been both painters and lamas for five generations, and apprenticeship begins at a very young age.

There are no trees in Dolpo, so paper and canvases that are stretched on wooden frames called *tang-ka* are precious commodities. As a child, Tenzing Norbu drew on the ground itself, using his finger as a pencil. He drew until his index finger became sore. Later his father gave him a plank of wood that had been stained black, and he used it like a slate. He would smear the plank with yak butter and cover it with dried and ground earth or yak dung. Then he used a small stick to make the lines of his drawings appear in black.

At the age of eight, Tenzing Norbu went to live in a monastery where he learned to paint, pray and become a lama. Before he was twenty-one, he had never left the high valleys of Dolpo, and had never seen a tree.

Tenzing Norbu now lives in Kathmandu, the capital of Nepal, where he teaches painting and creates *tang-ka* that trace the history of Dolpo and the salt trade, the main activity of the region. He has four children. For three months each year he returns to his monastery in Dolpo to visit his family and find inspiration for his paintings.

Tenzing Norbu is an extremely gifted artist who has contributed greatly to the development of art in Nepal, but he is also a lama, a priest of his people.